3 MINUTE
BEDTIME STORIES

This book belongs to

....

3 MINUTE
BEDTIME STORIES

Written by Nicola Baxter

Illustrated by Andy Everitt-Stewart

BACK
PACK
BOOKS

This 2004 edition published by Backpack Books
by arrangement with Bookmart Ltd

Backpack Books, Inc.
122 Fifth Avenue
New York, NY 10011

ISBN 0-7607-6059-4

Printed and bound in Singapore

M 1 3 5 7 9 10 8 6 4 2

Produced for Bookmart Limited by
Nicola Baxter
PO Box 215, Framingham Earl,
Norwich Norfolk NR14 7UR

Designer: Amanda Hawkes
Production designer: Amy Barton

Contents

The Dragon

At school, Josh's teacher read the class a story about a dragon. It was very exciting. Josh couldn't think about anything else all day. That night he even had a dream about a dragon. It was frightening and not frightening at the same time.

The next morning Josh was eating his breakfast in the kitchen when he suddenly grabbed his dad's arm, spilling cereal everywhere.

"Look, Dad!" he cried. "There's a dragon in the garden!"

Dad looked out. He saw a little smoke drifting over the fence. "It's just Jim next door having a bonfire," he said. "Look at the state of my sweater!"

Later, Dad went out to cut the grass. Josh followed him. Suddenly, Josh yelled, "Dad! Look at this!"

Dad dropped grass cuttings all over the lawn. Josh was staring at the path. "Dragon footprints!" he cried.

Dad looked and frowned. "Don't be silly," he said. "That's next-door's cat scratching the path again. Now look at the mess on the lawn!"

Josh wasn't convinced. He was pretty sure he saw dragon scratch marks on the fence (though it *could* have been the cat) and dragon bite marks on the cabbages (though it *could* have been slugs). Dad said that if he heard another word about dragons, he might go mad.

Josh went inside. *Thud! Thud!* Could it be a you-know-what?

No, it was just his mother moving the furniture. Josh laughed. He decided to stop thinking about dragons and play in his room instead. He was in for a surprise....

The New Village

Once upon a time there was a friendly giant. He lived in a huge castle on a hill. At the bottom of the hill there was a village. The people in the village were the same size as you and me, but they got on pretty well with the giant. He was always careful to keep to the path up the hillside so that his big boots didn't trample the fields around the village.

One day, the giant went to visit a friend. When he was ready to come home, it was already dark.

"I'll lend you a lantern," said his friend.

So the giant set out with his lantern. The moon was shining. It was easy to see the way. But as the giant walked, a storm blew up. Clouds covered the moon. The wind and rain put out the lantern. Suddenly it was wet and cold and very, very dark.

The giant hurried to get home to his warm castle, but he really couldn't see where he was going. *Crunch!* He put his big foot on something in the dark. *Crunch! Crunch!* At last, the giant reached his home and his giant-sized bed.

In the morning, he woke to hear a faint wailing sound.
At the bottom of the hill, the people who were the
same size as you and me were in a terrible state.

"In the night," they told the giant, "the storm
flattened most of the village. Luckily, no one
was hurt, as we were at a party further down
the valley. But look at our homes! Winter
is coming, and we have nowhere to live."

The giant looked at the flattened village.
He didn't think the storm had done this.
He felt dreadful.

"Let me help," he said. But his huge fingers
were too clumsy to build little houses.
He just got in the way. What could he do?

Then the giant had a good idea.
"My castle is very big," he said.
"There would be room for all of
you while you rebuild your village."

But that is not quite what happened. The villagers *did* go to stay with the
giant, but they were so warm and comfortable in the castle that they never
did rebuild their village! And the villagers and the giant lived happily
together ever after.

The Magic Potato

Once upon a time there was a lazy little elf. His mother did everything for him. She cooked him three big meals every day (and one or two snacks in between). You will not be surprised to know that he was also quite a plump little elf!

One day, the elf's mother had to go to visit her sister, who was ill. "You'll be fine," she told her son. "I know you love potatoes, so I've left you a big bag in the kitchen. All you have to do is to put them in the oven for delicious baked potatoes."

The elf did as she said. It was quite easy, and for several weeks he ate baked potatoes for nearly every meal. That was a mistake. Soon, there were only a few potatoes left in the bottom of the bag.

The elf went to the market to buy some more. He knew that was what his mother did when things ran out. But the stallkeepers shook their heads. Oh no, there are no potatoes to be had anywhere, they said. The elf was worried. He telephoned his mother.

"Do not eat the last potatoes," she said. "They are magic. Put them in the ground and wait to see what happens."

The elf was very puzzled, but he did what she said. He knew that his mother's father's sister's cousin had been a fairy, so there was a little magic in the family.

The next morning, there were green shoots where he had planted the potatoes. And by lunchtime, there were tiny yellow flowers as well. By the evening, the leaves and flowers had started to die.

The elf phoned his mother again. He was beginning to feel very hungry. "Well done," she replied. "Now dig where the potato plants grew."

The little elf dug and found, to his amazement, dozens and dozens of potatoes. "It's magic!" he told his mother that evening as he sat, happily full, by the phone.

"It is magic," said his mother, "but anyone can do it. It just happens faster with a fairy in the family."

The elf went to bed, and when he woke up, he had a brilliant idea. He grew some more potatoes and took them to the market! Everyone wanted to buy them. By the time his mother came home, the little elf was happier, fitter and richer than he had ever been before. And he wasn't lazy any more. Maybe that was the real magic!

Wizard Muddle

There was once a bad wizard called Billings. He didn't mean to be bad, but his spells always went wrong. When Mrs. Mumble wanted to make her vegetables grow, his spell made her hair grow! Mr. Hoggle wanted a cure for his headache, but Wizard Billings turned him into a frog!

On the whole, people tried not to ask for Wizard Billings's help, but there are some things you really do need a wizard for. When little Bubble's kitten went missing and couldn't be found, his granny took the little boy to the wizard. There was nothing left to try.

Wizard Billings listened to Bubble's troubles and promised that he could help. "Now where did I put that potion?" he muttered.

Bubble's granny looked around the wizard's cave. It was in a terrible mess. There were bottles and jars everywhere.

Wizard Billings peered at some pink liquid in a tall, thin bottle. "Ah, this is the one," he said.

Granny stopped him just in time. "This bottle has a label that says, 'Potion for turning things purple!'" she said. "That's not what we need! Can't you see?"

Wizard Billings shifted uncomfortably, and Granny suddenly understood a great deal.

"Wizard Billings, come with me!" she cried.

She led the wizard and Bubble down the hillside to the office of Miss Blink, the optician.

When Wizard Billings came out half an hour later, he was wearing a smart pair of glasses and grinning broadly.

"I didn't realize I needed glasses," he said. "How much clearer everything is now. In fact, what is that small, furry thing at the top of that tree?"

"My kitten!" cried Bubble. "Oh no, he's stuck!"

"No problem," cried the wizard. He hurried back to his cave and found a green potion that would do the trick. (On the label, it said, "Mixture for bringing kittens down from trees. Do not use on cows.")

Things are much happier in Wizard Billings's village now. Bubble has his kitten back, the vegetables are huge, and Mr. Hoggle is no longer a frog. Just in case, Wizard Billings has made up a big bottle of potion with a label in huge letters. It says:

Potion for finding lost glasses

The Dancing Elephant

Cheeky Monkey swung through the jungle. He spotted his friend Enormous Elephant. "See you tomorrow, Enormous!" shouted Cheeky as he passed.

"Tomorrow?" trumpeted the elephant. "Why, what's happening tomorrow?"

"It's Stripy Tiger's birthday party, of course!" yelled Cheeky, and he disappeared into the trees.

Enormous Elephant was stunned. He hadn't been invited to Stripy's party. Elephants never forget, so he was very sure. But Stripy was one of the elephant's oldest friends. How could he have been left out?

Enormous went home and didn't feel like eating his supper. His mother was worried. Enormous was always hungry! In the end, the elephant told her what had happened.

"That's very strange," said his mother. "I think it must be a mistake. I'll have a little word with Mrs. Tiger."

While Enormous slept, Mrs. Elephant did just what she had promised. She was surprised by the answer.

"That's right," said Mrs. Tiger. "We didn't invite Enormous."

"But why? He's so upset!" cried Mrs. Elephant.

"Oh dear. You see, there are a lot of little ones coming," explained her friend, "and it's a *dancing* party!"

Now Mrs. Elephant understood. When Enormous danced, the whole jungle shook, and certainly it was dangerous for little animals anywhere near his huge feet. But she did feel sorry for her son. It wasn't his fault his feet were so big.

"I've had an idea," she told Mrs. Tiger.

When Stripy's mother heard the idea, she was delighted.

The next day, Enormous went happily along to the party with all his friends. When the dancing started, some of the animals looked anxiously at Enormous, but the huge animal smiled. "Dancing isn't just about moving your feet," he said. "I can do a kind of dancing that none of you can!"

"What do you mean?" cried his friends.

"I mean *trunk* dancing!" laughed Enormous. And he swayed and wiggled his trunk to the music in the most wonderful way, without ever moving his feet at all.

Everyone agreed it was the best party ever, and Enormous's trunk dancing was fantastic, especially when he lifted up the birthday tiger. Then the party really went with a swing!

Up, Up and Away!

When Farmer Harris heard that a little boy in the village needed money for a special chair to help him get around, he was determined to help. He decided to have an Open Day on his farm.

For weeks, Farmer Harris got ready for the big day. He even polished his tractor and trailer so he could give rides around the farm.

He persuaded his sister to run a cake stall, and made lots of lemonade. He planned a treasure hunt for the older children. But what about the little ones? Farmer Harris got in touch with a shop in town and persuaded them to bring hundreds of helium-filled balloons at a very reasonable price.

When the day arrived, the farmer was amazed by how many people attended. He stood near the gate, holding huge bunches of balloons in each hand, welcoming all who came, young and old.

Farmer Harris was especially pleased when the little boy who needed the chair arrived in his mother's arms.

"Can we have a photo?"
called a newspaper reporter.
"Give him a balloon.
It will look great."

But Farmer Harris was so keen
to be kind that he didn't give
just one balloon. He gave Sean
two whole bunches of balloons!

Sean was a very small boy. As soon
as he grabbed the balloons, he
started to rise up into the air!

"Help!" cried his mother.

"Help!" cried Farmer Harris.

"Wheee!" cried Sean. "This is FUN!"

The grown-ups watched in
amazement as Sean floated off over
the farm. They chased him through the farmyard … and through
the fields (scaring the scarecrow) … and over the hills (surprising
the sheep) … and back down the lane to the barnyard. This time,
some of the balloons caught on the weathervane, leaving Sean
sitting on top of the roof!

Farmer Harris rushed out with his long ladder and soon
rescued the little boy. He carried him over to his family.

"I'm so, so sorry…," he began.

But Sean's mother smiled. "Look at his face," she said.
"He's had a wonderful adventure. Let's not say another word."

But there *was* another word to say to Farmer Harris; "Thanks!" The
picture of Sean flying appeared in every newspaper in the country, and
enough money arrived to buy chairs for hundreds of children like him.

The Christmas Tree

Christy lived in a big house. There was a hallway with a huge staircase winding up from it. At Christmas, Christy's dad brought in an enormous Christmas tree that stretched nearly to the ceiling far above. It was decorated with all sorts of shining ornaments and tinsel. It looked wonderful. Christy didn't know anyone who had such a big and beautiful tree.

One year, Christy's dad told her that the whole family was going to move for a while. He had a job at a college far away. It wasn't for ever, but it was too far to travel backwards and forwards.

"We'll live in a little flat for a year," said Dad. "It will be fun."

And it was fun, until it came to Christmas. One morning, Christy came down to breakfast to find a tiny little tree sitting on a small table.

"We haven't got room for a big tree," said her mother, "but this little one is fun, isn't it?"

Christy looked at the tiny tree in disgust. "That's not a tree," she said. "It's just silly. I want a big tree like the one we had last year."

Outside the window, there was a huge pine tree. "That's the kind of tree we want," said Christy, pointing.

"It wouldn't fit in here!" laughed her mother. "It wouldn't even come through the door. And anyway, we haven't got any of our decorations or lights here."

But she found it hard to forget Christy's disappointed face, and on Christmas Eve, she had an idea. Christy's dad borrowed a ladder and tied all sorts of things to the tree outside. There were seeds and nuts and bright red apples. There were garlands of peanuts in their shells threaded together and upsidedown coconut shells. It looked rather strange.

"Do you think this will work?" asked Dad.

"Wait and see," smiled Christy's mother.

On Christmas Day, when Christy looked out of the window, the tree was filled with birds and squirrels, all happily pecking and nibbling away.

"It's even better than our tree back at home!" cried Christy.

So always after that, Christy's family had two Christmas trees, an indoor one and an outdoor one. You might like to try it, too.

One Fish, Two Fish

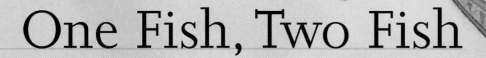

There was once a little orange fish who lived in the warm blue waters of the Indian Ocean. One day he was playing hide-and-seek with his mother in and out of the coral.

"Count to ten," said his mother, "then come and find me."

So the little fish counted out loud. "One, two, three, six, eight, ten! I'm coming!"

"Hey," said the mother fish, "that's not right! Start again!"

So the little fish put his fins over his eyes and began, "One, two, three, four, nine, seven, ten! Coming!"

When he looked up, his mother was not hiding. "Little fish," she said firmly, "we need to do some work on your counting. That wasn't right at all. Look, there are lots of friends to count right here."

"One crawly crab!" cried the little fish. "Two yellow fish! Now what?"

"Three of us!" cried his mother. "You, me and Dad, who is snoozing behind that rock. Look!"

"Three orange fish!" cried the little one. "Er…."

"It's simple," said his mother. "Four little starfish, five wiggly eels, six striped swimming fish, seven purple puffer fish, eight legs on Oscar octopus, nine speedy red fish, and ten tiny turtles. Now you try."

The little fish counted, "One crawly crab, two yellow fish, three orange fish, four little starfish … oh no! The wiggly eels are wiggling! I can't count them when they're moving. And the six striped swimming fish are worse!"

The little fish's mother saw that it was true. "Just a minute," she said.

The next moment, the little fish heard, "Smile, please!" and not long after, his proud parents brought him a beautiful big photograph of the undersea world. He could easily count now that everyone was still. Can you help him?

The Hungry Bear

There was once a bear who lived in a cave in a forest. He was a very nice bear and never troubled anyone except once a year in the springtime. You see, that was when he woke up from his winter's sleep, and when he woke up he was very, very hungry. That made everyone else very, very worried.

One year, on the first fine day of spring, the bear woke up and stretched. He had only one thing on his mind: food! He stomped off down the forest path.

The first creature he met was a squirrel.

"I'm going to eat you!" said the bear. And he did! But he was in such a hurry that he swallowed the squirrel whole, and he could feel the little animal scampering up and down inside him as he walked along.

Next he came to a lane, where a cat was chasing a mouse. In one gulp, the bear ate the cat and the mouse! But the cat was still chasing the mouse inside the bear. It felt very funny.

The bear was still hungry, and when he saw a field of sheep, he jumped over the fence and swallowed the nearest one. But the sheep was a ram. With his big horns he kept butting the bear from inside! Ouch!

By the time a little boy came walking down the lane, the bear was feeling rather poorly and sitting down.

The boy was not frightened. He put his hands on his hips and said firmly, "It's your own fault, you know. Come with me. I think I can help."

The boy ran off, leaving the bear to trot after him. It was not very comfortable, and as the bear jogged up and down, the big ram jumped right out of his mouth. That felt much better. Then, as the bear followed the boy over a fence, the cat and the mouse jumped out. Aaah! That was better still.

Last of all, as the boy and the bear came tumbling down a hill, the squirrel jumped out. Phew! The bear felt fine except … he was very hungry again!

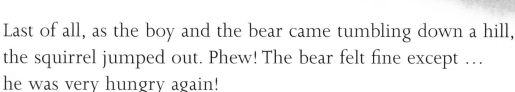

The boy threw open the doors of a big barn. Inside, the villagers had filled a table with pies and cakes! With a growl of delight, the bear rushed in and began to eat.

"Each year," said the boy, "we'll make you lots of good things to eat at the beginning of spring, if you promise not to eat our cats or dogs or sheep or cows! Is it a deal?"

The bear couldn't say a word. His mouth was too full of pies and cakes. But, picking up another pie, he nodded his head. He has never been a problem since.

Patty Pig

Patty Pig was the youngest of eight brothers and sisters. They were all pink, cheeky pigs with curly tails. It was very hard to tell them apart, but Mamma Pig and Papa Pig always seemed to manage it.

Still Patty Pig wasn't happy. "I want to be different," she muttered to herself.

One day, Patty Pig was munching some carrots in the barnyard when she saw something interesting. It was a huge, muddy puddle!

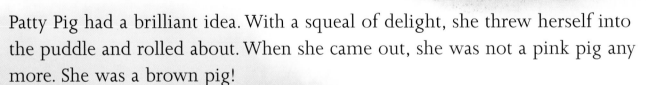

Patty Pig had a brilliant idea. With a squeal of delight, she threw herself into the puddle and rolled about. When she came out, she was not a pink pig any more. She was a brown pig!

"Hah!" said Patty Pig. "Now I'm different!"

But behind her she suddenly heard a lot more squeals of delight. Her brothers and sisters, seeing their muddy sister, thought rolling in the puddle was a great idea. In seconds, there were eight brown piglets in the yard.

Patty Pig frowned. Then she grinned.
She rushed over to the duckpond and
threw herself in with a massive SPLASH!

When she came out, all the mud was gone.
"Hah! I'm the only pink piglet," she giggled.

You can guess what happened next.
With deafening squeals and splashes
and sploshes everywhere, the seven
muddy piglets also jumped into the pond.
Soon, eight pink piglets were back in the yard.

Patty Pig was upset. Mamma Pig and Papa Pig noticed
and asked her what was the matter. Poor Patty explained.

Then Mamma and
Papa laughed out
loud. "But Patty,"
they cried, "you *are*
different. You don't
need to worry
about that at all!"

"How?" sniffed
Patty Pig.

"You are different
because, although
you were born last,
you are *always* the
first to do anything
new. You are a *very*
special piglet."

You are very special, too! Why don't you ask the grown-up
who is sharing this book with you just how special you are?

The Mouse in the Clock

There was once a mouse who lived in a grandfather clock. The clock stood in a corner of the hall of a very old house. It hadn't worked for years. Inside the clock, the little mouse had plenty of room to run about and a snug little space at the top, behind the face, where she slept. She was very happy in her home.

One day the old man who lived in the house had a visit from his sister. She was a bossy woman.

"Alfred! You should have that clock mended," she said.

The old man knew that she would go on and on and on until she got her way, so the next day he called a clock-mender.

The man who came to look at the clock smiled. "This is a fine old clock," he said, "and there probably isn't much wrong with it. I might be able to have it working for you by lunchtime."

He opened the case, and the little mouse scurried out of a hole at the back and hid under the stairs.

It didn't take the man long to get the clock working.

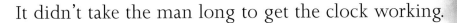

"I think you've had mice in here," he told the old man. "You'll need to watch that."

Well before lunchtime, the clock-mender was gone, and the little mouse crept back into her home. It felt very different. For a start, there was the loud ticking. *Tick, tick, tick, tick....* It went on and on. Then there was a big metal thing swinging dangerously backwards and forwards in the case. It was the pendulum, but the little mouse didn't know that.

Worse was to come. At a quarter past eleven, the clock struck. *Ding, dong, ding, dong, ding, dong, ding, dong!* At half past, it chimed the same tune twice. At a quarter to the hour, the chimes happened three times! But at twelve o'clock there was a dreadful noise. DONG! DONG! DONG! DONG! DONG! DONG! DONG! DONG! DONG! DONG! DONG! DONG!

The little mouse was so unhappy. How could she live like this? Forgetting to hide, she sat outside the clock with her paws over her ears. Suddenly, she realized the old man was standing next to her.

"It's awful," he said. "I've loved the peace of this house for seventy years, and now it's ruined. I can't stand it!"

He looked down and noticed the little mouse. A look of understanding came over his face. "This can be our secret," he whispered. And he carefully opened the clock's case, took out the long metal pendulum, and walked quietly away with it.

That night, everyone in the huge old house was happy again.

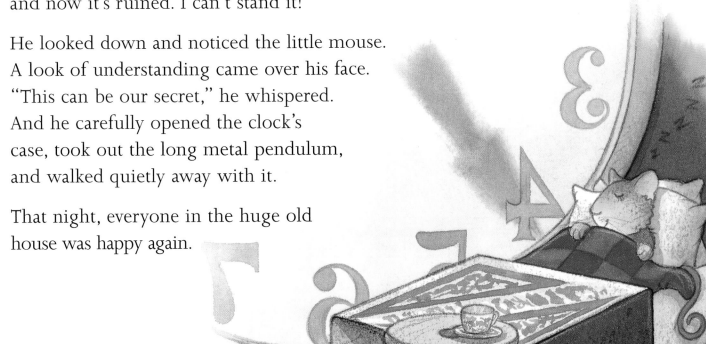

The Magic Eggs

There was once a farmer who had a fat, brown hen called Mildred. She laid beautiful white eggs, which the farmer enjoyed every day for his breakfast.

One morning, when he went to see Mildred for his breakfast egg, the farmer had a big surprise.

"Certainly not!" said the hen (who usually only said, "Cluck!") She gave the farmer a sharp peck on the hand and put her beak in the air.

"What's going on here?" said the farmer crossly. "I won't have a hen telling me what to do! Give me that egg!"

"No!" said the hen. "This is a magic egg. I can't give it to you."

The farmer decided not to risk another peck. He went back into the farmhouse and thought about what Mildred had said. A magic egg? There were no such things! On the other hand, he hadn't thought there were talking hens, either.

All that day, the farmer thought and thought. He remembered all the stories he had ever heard about magic when he was a boy. He couldn't think of any where magic was a *bad* thing. Perhaps the egg would give him three wishes!

The next day, Mildred again refused to let the farmer take an egg. "This one is magic, too," she said. Now she was sitting on two of them.

Two magic eggs! Could that mean (the farmer had to count on his fingers) *six* wishes?

The next day, and the next day, and the day after that, the same thing happened. Soon Mildred was sitting on six magic eggs, and the farmer had done lots of sums on bits of paper and worked out that he had eighteen wishes to come.

"I'm going to be rich!" he crowed. "I'm going to have a beautiful wife, and three fine sons, and three lovely daughters. I'm going to have a huge farm, and a fine horse to take me to church on Sundays. I'm going to have new suits of clothes and the best boots in the country. A famous artist will paint my portrait. I'll have dancing lessons. I'll … I'll …." But the farmer couldn't think of any more wishes, though he still had eight left.

Three weeks later, the farmer had a shock. Each one of Mildred's eggs hatched … and out hopped eight fluffy chicks!

The farmer was furious, but Mildred smiled. She thought those eggs had been pretty magical after all. What do you think?

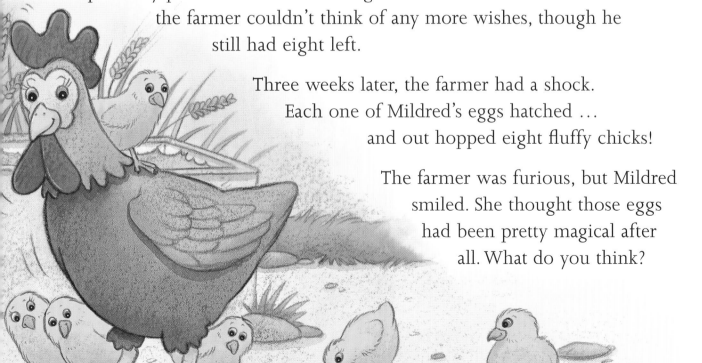

The Scarecrow

Rufus was excited. His village was holding a scarecrow competition. The idea was that each family would make a scarecrow and put it up in the front garden. The judges would walk through the village and choose a winner.

Rufus's dad grew vegetables for a living, so he knew a lot about scarecrows. Rufus was sure he would win. He found two stout branches in the hedgerow and tied them into a cross-shape with some string. Then he pushed the longest branch into the ground and fixed a big turnip on the top to make a head.

Rufus felt he had made a great start. Now all he had to do was to find some clothes for his scarecrow. That should be easy.

It wasn't. "Can I have your old hat for my scarecrow?" Rufus asked his dad.

"Certainly not," said Dad. "I'm still wearing it."

"What about your old jacket?"

"What, my nearly-new jacket with the small tear in the sleeve?" Dad replied. "You must be joking!"

It was the same when Rufus asked about trousers, a scarf, and an old pair of wellies.

"I need those wellies," said Dad firmly, "even though I don't wear them any more. You never know when they might come in handy."

Rufus was desperate. He even tried to find some old clothes of his own to use, but they were much too small. Grandad was no good either. He wanted to hang on to his old suits and shoes.

"Now you know where your dad gets it from!" grinned Rufus's mother. "Let me have a think."

When she spoke to him the next day, Rufus wanted to cry. "That's not right at all," he said. "Everyone will laugh!"

But he didn't have any choice, so Rufus dressed his scarecrow in a pair of tights stuffed with straw, a pair of green shoes, an orange and pink skirt, a yellow and blue jumper (also stuffed with straw), a red, curly wig, and a huge, flowery hat that his mother had once worn to a wedding. His was the only female scarecrow, and he thought it looked *awful*.

But later that week, the judges came around. "A clear winner!" laughed one of them. "I'm sure this lady's dreadful fashion sense would frighten any crow!"

"Well, really!" said Rufus's mother. But she said it very quietly indeed.

The Crown Crisis

There was once a princess who loved to play outside with all her bird and animal friends. She liked this much better than pretty clothes and jewels.

One day, when she was having a wonderful game chasing some baby bunnies through the forest, her golden crown got caught on a tree. The princess didn't even notice it was missing until she sat down to rest an hour later.

"Oh no!" she cried. "What will the king and queen say! I must find it!" But although she looked hard, she couldn't remember at all where she had been. The forest was very large, and the crown wasn't.

At last, the princess started to cry. "Don't worry," said a little bird. "I can build beautiful nests from twigs and leaves. I'll make you a new crown."

The little bird worked hard, and the crown fitted beautifully. But when the princess looked at herself in a forest pool, she started to cry again. "It's all stiff and brown," she sobbed. "I look as if I've got a bird's nest on my head!"

"Don't worry," croaked a green frog in the pool. "I can make something that will glisten and glitter, just like your real crown. Wait just a minute." He dived down to the bottom of the pool and came up with a shining, glittering crown! Water droplets shone on it like diamonds but … it was made of slimy pondweed! The princess shuddered and began to cry again.

Now all this time, one bright-eyed bird had kept quiet. He knew exactly where the princess's real crown was, for his sharp eyes had spotted its sparkle among the leaves.

The magpie loved anything shiny or glittering. He had planned to get the crown later and keep it for himself. Even *his* greedy heart was touched, however, by the princess's tears. Without a word, he flew off to get the crown.

When the princess saw the crown in the magpie's beak, she almost started crying again … with joy this time! Instead, she thanked the magpie and promised that she would never forget him, which is why, on her coat of arms, a cheeky black and white bird has pride of place!

The Kite Tangle

When Grandad came to visit, he always brought presents for Hattie, Jack, Kizzy and Shane. That should have been a good thing, but instead it usually led to arguments. Hattie said Jack's present was bigger. Shane wanted the book that Kizzy had been given. Grandad got fed up. "Next time I come," he said, "I'm going to bring you all exactly the same present. Then there'll be no quarrelling."

And that's just what he did … well, nearly. Grandad brought each of the four children a beautiful, bright kite! Each was exactly the same except for one thing. One was red. One was blue. One was green and one was yellow.

You can guess what happened.

"I'll have the red one!" cried Kizzy.

"No! I want the red one!" Jack yelled.

"That's not fair! I want it!" said Shane.

"I've already got my hand on it," said Jack.

Grandad looked grim. "This is hopeless," he said. "Put on your hats and coats, all of you, and your gloves, too. It's a lovely windy day but it's very cold. I'll decide who is having what as we walk up the hill."

On top of the hill, the children were soon having a wonderful time flying their kites, and there were no arguments at all! Clever Grandad! Can you follow the strings to work out how he decided who had which kite?

Where's That Book?

Professor Puffle was the wisest elf in Elfland. He knew almost everything there was to know, and if there was something he wasn't sure about, he looked it up in one of his books.

Professor Puffle had rooms and rooms full of books. Luckily, he was a very tidy elf, and he had a special book called a catalogue. It listed all the books in his library and told him just where to find them.

But the time came when the professor's little toadstool house simply wasn't big enough for all his books. He would have to move. Luckily, he soon found just the thing. It was a hollow tree-trunk. There was plenty of space in the tall trunk for hundreds of bookshelves.

"But how will I reach them?" wondered Professor Puffle.

Bangle Elf, the carpenter, had the answer. "When I build your bookshelves, I will also make you a basket on a rope," she said. "You will be able to pull yourself up and down and lean across to reach any book you like."

It sounded like an excellent plan. The very next day, while Professor Puffle was out visiting friends, she and her helpers were very busy indeed.

When the professor came home that afternoon, all the shelves were finished, and there were books stretching up towards the ceiling far, far above.

"It's wonderful," said the professor faintly. "But … er … did you put my books in order?"

There was a silence. The books were all muddled up!

"Don't worry, my friends," said the professor at last. "It was kind of you to help. I'll sort all the books out. First, I need to find my catalogue. It is blue with orange stripes."

Can you help to find the professor's special book, so that he can start to sort out his library?

Polly's Party

Polly was very excited. It was her friend Amy's birthday. She was having a big party, and Polly wanted to be the prettiest girl there.

After lunch, Polly disappeared into her bedroom.

"It's a bit early to start getting ready, Polly!" called her mother, but Polly didn't listen. She knew it might take a long time to decide what to wear.

Polly was lucky. She had lots of pretty clothes. First she tried on her blue dress with ribbons. It looked lovely. But what if there was lots of dancing? The ribbons might get in the way.

Polly tried on her purple velvet trousers and a sparkly pink top. Just right for dancing. But what if all the other girls were wearing dresses?

Polly put on a short, flowery skirt and a top with frills around the sleeves. That was good, too, but was it quite smart enough for a party?

Polly had an idea. In a box on top of her cupboard was the bridesmaid's dress she had worn when her aunty got married the year before. It was absolutely beautiful, in blue satin, with little pearl flowers on the top part.

Polly carefully pulled the dress out of the box and over her head. Oh dear! The party girl had grown in the last year, but the dress hadn't. It was much too tight to wear.

After that, Polly tried on three more dresses. None of them was right. When her mother came up to see how she was getting on, she found Polly sitting in the middle of a huge pile of clothes, crying.

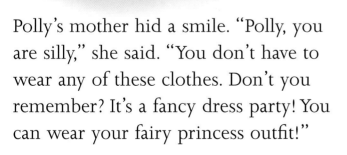

"Whatever is the matter?" she asked. "And what is all this mess?"

Polly told her. "I haven't got anything to wear!" she sobbed. "At least, not the right thing!"

Polly's mother hid a smile. "Polly, you are silly," she said. "You don't have to wear any of these clothes. Don't you remember? It's a fancy dress party! You can wear your fairy princess outfit!"

Polly looked lovely in her princess costume. But then I think she looked lovely in everything, don't you?

The Magic Flower

Once upon a time there was a very naughty little elf called Billo. He was much too little to learn how to do magic, but he wanted to try.

"How do you make magic fairy dust?" he asked Fairy Mary one day.

"That's a secret," said Fairy Mary. "It comes from a very special flower, deep in the Enchanted Wood. There is only one flower in the world that gives my kind of fairy dust, and only I know which one it is. Even when you find the flower, you can only shake out the dust if you have a silken purse to put it in."

Little Billo thought about this. He knew that fairy dust would help him to do all sorts of magic. The naughty elf decided to follow Fairy Mary next time she went into the Enchanted Wood to find the special flower.

Early one morning, Fairy Mary set out, carrying her silken purse. Billo tiptoed after her. It was fairly easy to follow her secretly through the wood because he could always hide behind a tree if she turned around.

After a long walk, Fairy Mary came to a big meadow. It was full of flowers. Fairy Mary walked right into the middle of it and shook a little blue flower into her purse. Then she hurried home.

Meanwhile, Billo had seen which flower she had shaken, and he didn't take his eyes off it. As soon as the fairy had gone, he hurried straight to it. But in his excitement, Billo had forgotten to bring a silk purse! He ran home to get one, but before he went, he popped his blue cap over the flower so he would know which one it was when he returned.

Billo got back to the meadow in record time, but he had a big surprise. Fairy Mary had done some clever magic of her own. Billo didn't find the fairy dust after all, which is probably just as well.

The Flying Rabbit

Bettina Bunny wanted to fly. I don't mean that she wanted to go in an aeroplane. I mean that she wanted to be able to flap her wings and soar into the air, just like the birds she watched from the roots of the old oak tree where she lived with her family.

There was only one problem. Bettina didn't *have* any wings.

"That's perfectly normal for a rabbit," said her father, when she complained. "You have four furry paws and two enormous ears. That should be enough for any bunny."

That gave Bettina an idea. Her ears really *were* enormous. They were just as big as some birds' wings. Surely she could fly with those?

Bettina went up to the top of a nearby hill and started flapping her ears. It was hard work. She tried hopping up and down as she did it. No good. Then she tried running down the hill while she flapped her ears. She fell over her feet before she got halfway down, and ended up rolling all the way to her home in the tree roots.

"Whatever are you doing, Bettina?" asked her mother, when she had picked herself up. "And why are your ears so droopy?"

"They're tired," said Bettina. And she explained what she had been doing.

Bettina's mother took her daughter outside and sat down with her.

"Now, Bettina," she said, "look at those cows over there. Can they fly?"

"No," said Bettina.

"That's because no one is good at everything, but everyone is good at something. Cows are good at giving milk and mooing. Birds are good at flying and singing. What are bunnies good at?"

"Jumping," said Bettina, looking a little happier.

"And cuddles," said her mother, putting her paws around her daughter.

Bettina liked jumping. She was glad she wasn't a bird after all. She didn't think they were very cuddly at all. She hugged her mother back and jumped away to play. Her ears looked happier, too!

Rowan's Pet

Rowan really wanted a pet, but he lived at the top of a tall building. His mother said there were rules about not being able to keep animals there. It didn't stop Rowan really wishing he could have one.

Things got worse when Rowan's preschool decided to have a fundraising day in the park. One of the events was to be a Grand Pet Show. All the children were really excited about bringing their pets. There were going to be prizes for the biggest pet, the fluffiest pet, the most unusual pet, the friendliest pet, and so on.

Rowan was determined not to be left out. On the day of the Pet Show, he marched into the tent where it was being held with a big sheet of paper rolled up.

The judges moved down the tables, making notes about each of the pets. There were fluffy rabbits, squiggly lizards, sleepy hamsters and chirping birds. One little girl had even brought worms in a kind of glass box filled with soil.

When they reached Rowan, the judges looked up kindly. "Can you show us your pet?" they asked.

"I can!" said Rowan proudly, and he unrolled a beautiful picture of a huge, floppy-eared rabbit with a pink nose. "His name is William," said Rowan.

"Well, that's a beautiful picture," said one of the judges, "but where is your rabbit?"

Rowan smiled. "In here," he said proudly, and he pointed to his head.

The judges looked at each other. "So he's an imaginary rabbit?" they asked. "He isn't a real rabbit?"

"He's very real to me," said Rowan firmly. "And what's more, he can do tricks. He can turn somersaults and jump high buildings. Sometimes he can do some magic, too."

"That's amazing," said the judges.

At the end of the Pet Show, it seemed as if every pet received a prize. The Smallest Mouse, the Wiggliest Worm, the Cheekiest Kitten all had ribbons. At last, only Rowan was left. "Honey, only real live pets can win prizes," whispered his mother. But she was wrong.

"And now we come to our final and most important prize," said the chief judge. "To Rowan goes the top prize for Most Extraordinary Pet." And everybody cheered.

Tomorrow, Tomorrow

Jackson knew that his birthday wasn't very far away. He couldn't wait. "Is it tomorrow, Mum?" he asked.

"No, honey," said his mother. "It's at the end of next week."

"You mean tomorrow, tomorrow, Mum?" Jackson was only a little boy. It was his way of describing the day after tomorrow.

Mum held up eight fingers in front of Jackson and counted them slowly. "It's in one day, two days, three days, four days, five days, six days, seven days, eight days!" she smiled.

"Oh," said Jackson, "you mean tomorrow, tomorrow, tomorrow, tomorrow, tomorrow, tomorrow, tomorrow, tomorrow!"

Mum counted on her fingers again. "Well, yes, that's right," she said, "but Jackson, that's not how we say it."

Jackson didn't hear. He had run off to tell his toys. Now he had the tomorrows straight in his head, he didn't need to listen any more.

The next day, when he bounced on Mum's tummy bright and early in the morning, Jackson said, "Guess what, Mum? My birthday's tomorrow, tomorrow, tomorrow, tomorrow, tomorrow, tomorrow, tomorrow!"

Sleepily, his mother worked it out. "That's right, Jackson," she yawned.

It was the same every morning. Jackson's mother awoke to a string of tomorrows, and Jackson grew more excited each day.

When there were four tomorrows left, Mum couldn't stand it any more. She bought a calendar for Jackson and put it up near his bed. She showed him how to cross off each day when it began, and she drew a big present on the day that was his birthday. For three days, she had peace in the mornings. Jackson could see his birthday was getting closer. He didn't need to keep reciting tomorrows.

The next day, the birthday came at last. Mum heard Jackson thudding down the landing on his way to jump on her in the morning.

"No more tomorrows, Jackson!" she laughed, as her son hurtled in.

"No!" yelled Jackson, as he landed *oomph* on her tummy as usual. "It's today, today, today, today, today, today, today, today, today, today, today, today…!"

The Big Little Brother

When Sarah told her friends she was going to have a little brother, they were very excited.

"I love babies," said Mia. "He'll have little tiny fingers and little tiny toes. Lovely!"

"Well…," began Sarah, but Gina rushed in.

"We could make a mobile to put over his cot," she said. "We could paint pretty fish … or little boats … or stars and a moon! I love making mobiles."

"I know, but…," said Sarah. Emma was bouncing up and down with excitement.

"We've got lots of toys from when my brother was born," she said. "He's at school now, so I'm sure you could have some of them for your baby. When is he going to be born?"

"Actually, I think…," Sarah started to speak, but Gina, looking wise and grown up broke in.

"Oh, I know about that," she said. "It won't be for a few months yet. Your mum doesn't look fat at all. After the holidays, I should think."

"Yes, that's right," said Sarah, "but…."

"Maybe he'll be born in September, like me!" cried Mia.

"Yes, his birthday will be September the fifth," Sarah yelled, "And his name will be Ben. But listen…."

It was no good. All the girls started chattering excitedly. They were very impressed that Sarah knew *exactly* when her brother's birthday would be.

The rest of the school year passed. It was holiday time. On the first day back at school after the holidays, Sarah came into the playground with a big grin on her face.

"He's here," she said. She was holding hands with a little boy of three with blonde hair and a shy smile. "This is Ben."

"But…," said Gina.

"But…," said Mia.

"But, I thought…," said Emma.

"You didn't let me tell you Ben was going to be my adopted brother," said Sarah. "And by the way, he really *loves* mobiles."

The Forgetful Fairy

"Fairy Fennel! Fairy Fennel!" called Mrs. Iggle. "I need your help right away!" She hammered on the door of Fairy Fennel's toadstool cottage.

Fairy Fennel opened her door with a worried look, but Mrs. Iggle didn't notice. "It's my Bert's back," she said. "He can't move a muscle. He's bent over like an ironing board, and he can't straighten up. We need you to come at once."

"Well…," began Fairy Fennel, but Mrs. Iggle wouldn't stop.

"He can't go on like this. How's he going to fit into bed? Come on, there's no time to lose!"

"But…," Fairy Fennel tried again.

"No buts," said Mrs. Iggle impatiently. "Put on your fairy cloak and come! Have a thought for my Bert!"

"You see…," Fairy Fennel tried to explain.

"I do see. I see a man in his prime bent double like an old fellow three times his age," protested her visitor. "I see someone who can't get his own shirt off. I see moaning and groaning all night that will keep me awake. For pity's sake, Fairy Fennel, pick up your wand and come!"

"That's just it," said Fairy Fennel, speaking very, very quickly. "Wand. Lost. Help? No. Sorry!"

"WHAT? Slow down!" cried Mrs. Iggle. At last the story came out. Fairy Fennel had lost her wand. She couldn't help anyone until she found it.

"You leave this to me," said Mrs. Iggle. "I'll go and get Bert to help look. We're good at finding things. I'll be back in a minute."

Sure enough, in a minute, Mrs. Iggle was back with Bert. She searched high up in Fairy Fennel's house, and Bert searched low down, for obvious reasons. Which of them do you think found the wand? Can you see it?

The Best Planet

One night, Annie Jones woke up to find a little green and pink person standing in the middle of her room. It (you really couldn't tell if it was a he or a she) seemed to glow, but not in a scary way. "Who are you?" gasped Annie.

"I'm Tig," said the person. "I come from a planet far, far, far, far, far…."

"Yes, yes, I see," Annie interrupted. "It's a long way away. What's your planet called?"

"Ig," said Tig.

Annie looked at her alien visitor with interest. "Have you visited any other planets?" she asked. "Earth is a bit boring. I was wondering if there was somewhere else I could live."

"Boring how?" said the alien.

"Horrible food at school," said Annie, "and a little brother who steals my crayons. Oh, and not being allowed to stay up and watch *Beryl, Magic Princess* because it's on too late. And helping tidy up on Saturdays."

"On Neopolita," said Tig, "there are four thousand different kinds of ice cream."

"That sounds good," grinned Annie. "I love ice cream after sausage and chips."

"Oh, there aren't any sausages and chips," said Tig. "Only ice cream. Maybe you'd prefer Merevil, where there are no little brothers."

"Magic!" cried Annie. "Can I have a little sister instead?"

"No, no. There are no little children at all. You would be the youngest by about sixty years," Tig explained. "On Palacia, where everyone is a magic princess, you would be, too. They have beautiful dresses and gorgeous hairstyles, and the prettiest shoes you've ever seen."

"Perfect!" cried Annie. "How do I get there? I can't wait to do magic and fight evil trolls and ride unicorns."

"Er, you won't be able to do that, I'm afraid," said Tig. "The princesses are only allowed to sit down all day, in case they mess up their dresses or their hair or their shoes."

Annie frowned. "I expect there is a planet where I wouldn't have to help my mother tidy up," she said.

"Oh yes," replied Tig. "On Varia, there are no mothers at all. Everyone there is a little sad, but you can't have everything."

The next morning, Annie jumped up and gave her little brother a hug, before tidying her bedroom. Her mother had to ask her if she was feeling all right.

"I'm just glad to be on this planet," said Annie, which made no sense to anyone else. But you understand, don't you?

The Apple Tree

Bobbie Bunny loved apples, and he was lucky enough to have a huge apple tree in his garden. When the summer sun was still warm, but there was a smell of woodsmoke in the air, the tree was full of apples. Each day they grew rosier and riper.

"Can we pick the apples today?" Bobbie asked his mother.

"Not yet," came the reply. "I'll tell you when."

But Bobbie couldn't wait. He pestered his mother at least ten times a day. "Is it time yet? They look very ripe to me," he said. "Apples can get too ripe, you know."

But the reply was always the same. "Not yet. I'll tell you when."

Bobbie looked up at the tree. Could he perhaps climb up and just, well, test for himself if the apples were ready?

He soon found that he couldn't. Bunnies are very good at hopping and digging. They are very bad at climbing trees. Mrs. Bunny kept the ladder locked up in the shed where little paws couldn't reach it.

In the afternoons, after school, Bobbie could only think of the apples. One day, he told his mother, "I don't care what you say. I'm going to sit under the apple tree until the apples are ripe. Even if it takes days and days and days."

"You'll get pretty cold and hungry," said his mother, "but it's up to you."

So Bobbie went to sit under the apple tree. He sat and he sat, looking up at the apples hanging high above him. At last, as the sun began to sink in the sky, he fell asleep.

Boink!

Something thwacked Bobbie on the nose! He jumped to his feet and looked around. Whatever had happened? His mother, coming out of the house at that moment, laughed.

"Bobbie," she said, "I said I would tell you when, but the tree has done it for me. The apples are ready!"

That night, Bobbie went to bed a very happy bunny. He didn't even think about his sore nose with a tummy full of the sweetest, juiciest apples he had ever tasted.

The Rainbow River

Long ago and far away there lived a boy who had never seen rain. He lived in a warm country, full of fruit and flowers, birds and animals, but behind his valley, mountains rose up steep and high. Rain did not fall on his side of the mountains.

Now almost everyone in the valley had lived there all their lives. They did not know that there were places where there was rain and snow and hard, stinging hail.

It was different for the boy. He had an uncle who had journeyed to many lands. The uncle came back with wonderful stories of storms at sea, and he told the boy about something else, as well. He spoke of a beautiful bow in the sky, called a rainbow, that appeared when the sun shone and the rain came down at the same time.

From the moment he heard about it, the boy could not get rainbows out of his mind. He longed to see one, but he understood that while he stayed in the valley, he never would. And so he made plans to leave as soon as he was old enough.

But when he *was* old enough, the man (for he was no longer a boy) found that he could not go. His parents were old and needed help. Later on, he had a wife and family of his own. At last, he was too old himself to climb the mountains and find a rainbow in the world beyond.

But the river that flowed through the valley was a magic river. It knew the secrets of the old man's heart. On the day that he walked down to the river for the last time, the magic waters prepared a wonderful surprise for him. The river was suddenly full of bright little fish, and the old man was content at last as he sat by his rainbow river.

Train Trouble

The tiniest train was very excited. After lots of practice, today was the day he would be taking real passengers into town.

The stationmaster picked up his whistle. He had one last word with the tiniest train. "Now, remember," he said, "it's very important to keep to the timetable. Make sure you don't get held up. Whatever happens, keep going! You must reach Hilltown by five minutes past two exactly. Don't be late!"

"I understand," said the tiniest train. "Whoo, whoo! Here we go!"

The stationmaster blew his whistle. The train was off!

There were several passengers on the train already, and the tiniest train was surprised how much harder it was to chug along. Some of them were very big passengers!

As he came to the first station, the tiniest train looked anxiously up at the station clock. What if he was already late? Without hesitating he speeded up, not stopping at the station at all! "I must be on time," he puffed.

So it went on. At each station, the tiniest train was afraid that he was late. He pressed on, not stopping once, remembering what the stationmaster had said.

At last, panting and puffing, he came to Hilltown.

"Goodness me," said the stationmaster there. "I wasn't expecting you for another ten minutes!"

"But it's five minutes to two!" hooted the train.

"And you're due at five minutes past two!" cried the stationmaster. "Just a minute, my phone's ringing!"

It was lots of angry passengers along the way, who had seen the tiniest train dashing past and not been able to get on. There were quite a few cross faces on the train as well – people who had wanted to get off and couldn't!

The stationmaster had a few stern words with the tiniest train. "Passengers don't want a train to be late," he said, "but even a late train is better than no train at all."

This time the tiniest train listened hard. On his next trip he stopped at every station – and he was on time, too!

The Butterfly Ball

Ladybird was scuttling here and there. "Have all the invitations been sent?" she asked Caterpillar.

"Yes," sniffed Caterpillar, "but there wasn't one for me!"

"Next year, dear boy," said Ladybird soothingly. "It's butterflies only, I'm afraid, but your turn will come."

Each year the butterfly ball took place late one afternoon in the sunniest part of the border. Ladybird, who loved to be busy, was usually in charge. "Now I must rush," she cried, "to speak to the new butterflies about costumes."

Ladybird flew around the garden. "Remember, dear things," she said to each pair of butterflies she met, "there will be a prize for the loveliest couple as usual. Paint your wings as beautifully as you can. You may win!"

The day of the ball arrived at last. All the creepy-crawlies who were not invited hid under leaves and behind stalks to watch the arrival of the gorgeous butterflies in their painted party costumes. "Ooooh! Aaaaah!" gasped the other insects, as each pair of butterflies looked lovelier than the last. When the dancing began, the sight of dozens of fluttering, jewel-like wings was breathtaking.

Ladybird called for attention. "It is time for the judging of the Most Beautiful Butterfly Couple Contest," she cried. "Ladies and gentlemen, find your partners, please!"

Oh dear, the butterflies were hopelessly mixed up!
Can you help to sort them into their pairs?
And which pair of butterflies do you think should win the prize?

The White World

Bianca couldn't wait for her cousin Bruno to visit, but when he came she began to wish he would go home! Bianca lived in the icy, snowy Arctic. Bruno came from a wooded mountain much further south. His fur was brown, while Bianca's was as white as the world she lived in.

Bruno smiled when he hopped off his iceberg and said hello, but it was the last time. From then on, he moaned without stopping.

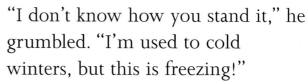

"I don't know how you stand it," he grumbled. "I'm used to cold winters, but this is freezing!"

Bianca opened her mouth to explain about her special, warm fur, but Bruno was off again.

"There's nothing to look at," he complained. "Just ice and snow. Where I come from there are trees and mountains, caves and rocks."

Bianca started to explain that polar bears had caves, too, dug out of the ice, but Bruno was still talking.

"No streams!" he groused. "I'm a champion fish-catcher. Look at these claws! How am I going to get any practice in this awful place?"

Bianca began to tell him about fishing through holes in the ice, and the beautiful fish to be found in the cold, deep waters beneath. Bruno would have none of it.

"There's nothing here," he announced, "that isn't better, bigger and more beautiful where I come from. I feel sorry for you, I really do."

Bianca was close to tears. Her mother, who had overheard some of what Bruno was saying looked up at the sky and smiled. "It will be dark in a moment," she said. "Let's sit out here for a moment and enjoy the stars."

"Stars!" snorted Bruno. "Nothing could be more lovely than stars over the mountains in my own land. I don't need to see them."

Suddenly, as happens in the Arctic, night fell. The dark, dark blue sky filled with twinkling points of light. "You see," said Bruno, "just ordinary stars. Oh!"

He sat with his mouth open, gazing up at the pink and red and blue and yellow and green and purple sky. It was the Northern Lights, giving an amazing show, like thousands of fireworks at once.

Bianca and her mother smiled at each other. They knew that there was nothing like this where Bruno came from. As for Bruno, he didn't say a word, which was the second amazing thing that had happened that night!

Ian's Invention

One rainy day, Ian didn't know what to do. "Why don't you make something?" suggested his dad. "You could use that old construction set Uncle Jim gave you."

Ian wasn't very keen at first, but when he had pulled all the pieces out of a battered cardboard box, he started to be interested. There were pipes, and cog-wheels, and elastic bands. There were funnels, and whistles, and axles. There were electric engines, and steam engines, and winding-up mechanisms. There were squiggly bits, and wiggly bits, and bits that looked so strange he wasn't sure *what* they were.

Ian started fitting pieces together. It was fun. Before long, his machine was as big as a chair.

By suppertime, it was bigger still. Ian gathered the family together. "I've invited you," he announced, "to my Grand Switch-On. This is the most remarkable machine the world has ever seen. Prepare to be amazed."

With a flourish, Ian flipped a big red switch. Dad knelt down on the floor for a better view. The dog hid behind Ian's little brother. His sister stepped back and peered over a cupboard door.

Splutter! Wooosh! Carrumph! Gurgle! Google! Whizz! Whir-bang! Eeeeeeeee! The machine began to jiggle. Cogs turned round. Water rushed down pipes and sprayed out in a fountain. Steam puffed out of a big green funnel. A funny hooting sound, like a cow stuck in a bathtub, began to make all the furniture shake.

"What on earth is it?" giggled Dad.

"It's ridiculous!" chortled Ian's sister, wiping tears from her eyes.

Ian's little brother sat down and laughed so hard his glasses fell off.

The dog rolled on the carpet, making a strange wheezing sound.

"But what does it do?" chuckled Dad. "Your machine is a failure, Ian. A machine that does nothing is no good."

But Ian smiled. "Not at all," he said. "My machine has been very successful. It's a Laughter Inducer. You all did laugh, didn't you?"

Waiting for William

Jake's mother told him she had a baby growing in her tummy. "When he comes out, he'll be your little brother," she said.

Jake couldn't wait. Each morning, when he woke up, he ran through to find his parents. "Will it be today?" he asked.

"No, no," said his mother. "Not yet. Growing babies takes a long time."

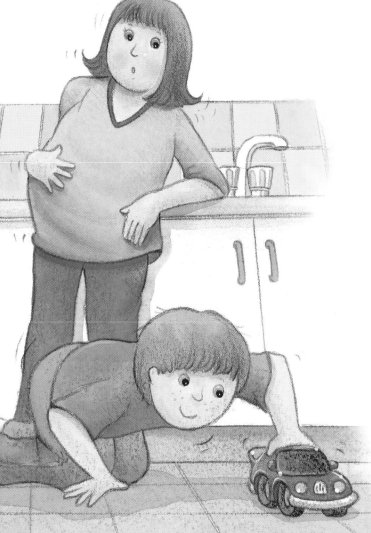

It did seem a very long time to Jake. Then, one morning, when he had almost given up believing in the baby, his mother suddenly said, "Ow! Oh! Jake, I'm going to call Aunty Pat. I think the baby's coming."

Aunty Pat came to look after Jake. Jake's mother walked up and down a lot and took a bath.

"Will it be here soon?" asked Jake.

"No, no," said his mother. "This bit often takes a long time, too."

At suppertime, Dad helped her into the car. "We're going to the hospital," he told Jake.

"But you can't!" wailed Jake. "You need to be here when the baby comes!"

Dad reminded Jake where the baby was! "You'll just have to wait," he said. "I'll ring you as soon as there's news."

Jake didn't want to go to bed, but in the end he was too sleepy to stay awake. "All this waiting makes me tired," he said.

In the morning, Jake woke up to find Aunty Pat sitting on his bed and smiling. "You've got a little brother, Jake," she said. "His name is William."

Jake wanted to go to see William straight away, but Aunty Pat said,
"No, we'll wait here. William will be home by lunchtime."
So Jake waited some more.

At last, he heard the car arrive. When his mother was settled on the couch, he had a chance to see William for the first time. He was perfect!

"He was worth waiting for," whispered Jake,
holding his brother's tiny hand.

"All good things are,"
smiled his mother.

The Dancing Shoes

"Princess Miranda, it's time for your dancing lesson!" called Madame Evadne. But Princess Miranda had other ideas.

"Dancing is boring," she said. "I don't want to have my lesson today. And I'm a princess, so I don't have to do anything I don't want to!"

Madame Evadne looked cross, but it was true. In Madame Evadne's opinion (well, in everyone in the palace's opinion), Princess Miranda was the rudest, laziest, most spoilt girl in the land, but she was also a princess. Madame Evadne curtseyed and went away.

The same thing soon began to happen whenever Madame Evadne came to teach dancing. As a result, Princess Miranda had no idea how to do the one-step, the two-step, or the Moravian Alpine Fling.

Princess Miranda grew up, as princesses do. And as princesses do, she spotted a prince she thought would make a very good husband.

"Well, there is only one thing to do," said the king, when his daughter told him (she was used to getting what she wanted, remember). "You will have to win his heart at the Royal Ball."

"How?" asked Miranda.

"By dancing like an angel," replied the king, sweeping away.

Princess Miranda looked grim. Then she scurried down into the dungeons where an evil old witch had been kept for several hundred years. The witch was bad but not stupid. In return for her freedom, she gave the princess what she asked for: a pair of magic slippers that would dance divinely all by themselves.

The day of the ball arrived. The prince arrived. Princess Miranda made her entrance. Then the dancing began. Princess Miranda put on the magic slippers and, goodness me, they worked! To everyone's surprise (especially Madame Evadne's), she danced beautifully.

Unfortunately, Miranda had not the slightest idea how to stop the slippers. When the prince asked to take her to supper, she danced on. When she began to feel hungry herself, the slippers wouldn't take her anywhere near the buffet. When she needed to visit the ladies' room, oh dear....

As far as I know, Princess Miranda is still dancing. Two people, though, did find a happy ending. Madame Evadne caught the eye of the prince. The prince caught the eye of Madame Evadne. They lived happily ever after.

Too Many Toys!

"Oooff!" Jack and Janna's mother landed with a thud. Luckily she fell straight onto the couch in their playroom, but she still wasn't very pleased. "How many times have I told you to put your toys away?" she said, glaring at the truck she had just fallen over. "Christmas is coming, and then there'll be even more toys! What are we to do then?"

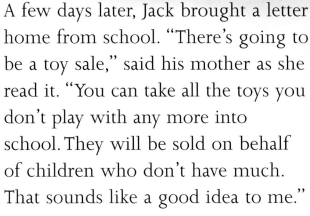

Jack and Janna grinned at the idea of Christmas, but they didn't want their mother to get any crosser. "We'll tidy up, we promise," they said, putting on their most angelic expressions.

A few days later, Jack brought a letter home from school. "There's going to be a toy sale," said his mother as she read it. "You can take all the toys you don't play with any more into school. They will be sold on behalf of children who don't have much. That sounds like a good idea to me."

Jack and Janna weren't so sure, but when all their friends began to bring toys into school, they became keener. By the end of the week, they had filled a big cardboard box with toys. Their mother was very happy.

She had a meeting on the day of the toy sale, so Gran came over to keep an eye on the children. "Please can we go to the sale at school, Gran?" asked Jack. "It's in ever such a good cause."

Gran agreed, and when she heard what the money from the sale would be used for, she gave Jack and Janna some extra pocket money to spend as well.

That night, Jack and Janna went to bed with happy smiles. "They've been good as gold," said Gran, when their mother came home. "And you'd be proud of the way they supported the school and poor children today."

"What exactly do you mean?" asked her daughter faintly. "No, I'd better go and see for myself."

It was only just possible to open the door to the playroom. Jack and Janna had bought back nearly all the toys they had taken to the sale … and quite a few more as well.

Gran laughed when she heard what had happened. "At least it's in a good cause," she said. And *everyone* had to agree.

Millie's Magic

Millie was a very sweet little fairy. But she wasn't very good at listening. In the middle of being told something, a dreamy look would come into her eyes.

"What did I just say, Millie?" her mother would ask. And Millie would smile charmingly and say, "I heard every word."

One day, Millie's mother had an appointment. It was a wing check-up. Fairies, you see, have wing check-ups just as we have check-ups for our teeth. It's very important that a fairy's wings work properly, especially if you are a busy mother with a naughty little fairy like Millie to look after.

"I need to wash my wings and get ready," said Millie's mother this particular day. "Could you wash up the lunch things, please? And just do it the human way, please. No magic. You haven't learnt to deal with bubbles yet, and they can be tricky."

Millie promised that she would, but in fact she had stopped listening after the words "wash up the lunch things." As soon as her mother had fluttered upstairs, she climbed onto a chair and said some magic words.

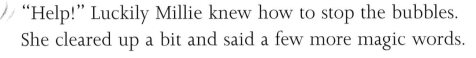

Woooosh! The plates and cups and bowls flew into the sink.

Wheeeee! The tap turned itself on.

Bliggle bloggle bling! Bubbles started to froth up alarmingly over the sink.

"Help!" Luckily Millie knew how to stop the bubbles. She cleared up a bit and said a few more magic words.

Woooosh! The clean plates and cups and bowls jumped out of the sink, twizzled in the air to get dry, and stacked themselves neatly on the table. They gleamed.

Millie clapped her hands with delight and went to get her coat.

A few minutes later, there was a yell from the kitchen.

"Millie!!! Come here at once! What have you done?"

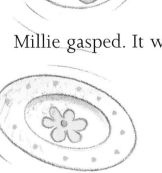

"I just did the washing up," said Millie.

"Isn't there something you've forgotten?" said her mother sharply. "When these dishes were dirty, they had a pattern of stars all over them. Now they're white! You've cleaned off everything, not just the food!"

Millie gasped. It was true. "I can fix it!" she cried.

"Don't even start!" said her mother, but it was too late. In seconds, one plate had a pattern of blue elephants. Another had red stripes. Another had yellow stars.

Do you think Millie's mother put things right? Do you always listen carefully?

The Hungry House

One morning, when Mr. Paulus went shopping, he left his front door open. His sister was coming to visit, so he was in a hurry.

Passers-by didn't notice the open door, but the house noticed them. It felt hungry. Yes, hungry. Let me explain….

Mr. Paulus was a professor. When he wasn't teaching, he had his nose in a book. Mr. Paulus was always so busy studying, he didn't have any friends. His sister came just once a year.

Mr. Paulus didn't pay attention to his house, either. He kept it clean, but it was years since he had painted it or bought a new carpet. So the house was hungry. It had an empty space inside where there should have been people on the sofas, and paintings on the walls, and delicious smells coming from the kitchen.

So what did the house do, with its door standing open like a big mouth? It ate a passing lady! Then it ate a little boy and his mother. And two grannies with hats on. And the chef from the café opposite. And a dog. After that, the house looked happier.

When Mr. Paulus arrived home, he was surprised to see his front door standing open. He was even more surprised to find that the house seemed somehow more warm and welcoming. He was very, very surprised to find six people and a dog chatting happily in his front room.

"I hope you don't mind," said the chef. "I made us some coffee and found some biscuits. None of us is quite sure how we came here, but we've so enjoyed getting to know each other."

"I brought you some flowers," said one of the grannies. "It was so good of you to invite us, although I can't remember that happening. I put them in a vase for you."

"I put up one of my pictures," said the little boy. "I hope you like it."

"You have a lovely house," said his mother.

Mr. Paulus looked around. It was true! Although he had never noticed in all these years, he did have a lovely house. Just at that moment, his sister arrived.

"Goodness," she said, "what have you done to the place, Albert? It looks wonderful. Oh, hello!"

"Allow me to introduce my friends," said Mr. Paulus, "or … er … perhaps they could introduce themselves."

Mr. Paulus's life changed from that day.
He was a much happier man.
And his house was much happier, too.
Make sure you look after your house, won't you? You never know what a hungry house will do!

They're Behind You!

When Rhiannon went to stay with her aunt, who was a farmer, she couldn't wait to see the animals. She was cross to find that her aunt seemed to want to give her a lecture first!

"You must never feed the animals," said her aunt, "unless I am there. You can really hurt an animal by giving it the wrong food. And you must never drop litter in the fields. Animals can be hurt if they eat that, as well. And you must never go near an animal who has a small baby, unless I am there. The mother might attack you if she thought you were going to hurt her baby."

After a while, Rhiannon stopped listening. She simply wanted to go outside, not listen to all this stuff. That is why she didn't hear the part about never, ever leaving gates open.

At last Rhiannon was free to run out into the farmyard. She went to see the baby pigs first of all. They were so sweet and squiggly that she just had to go inside to say hello. Of course, she completely forgot to shut the gate after her.

The sheep were gorgeous, too. Rhiannon loved the baby lambs and the baby lambs seemed to love her back. Rhiannon skipped out of the meadow like a baby lamb herself – and left the gate open.

The cows were very big and very friendly. They nuzzled up to Rhiannon with their warm breath and big brown eyes. Rhiannon got a little bit frightened and hurried off – leaving the gate open.

Rhiannon also visited the goats, the ducks, and the two little ponies in the back paddock.

At tea time, Rhiannon ran back down the lane to find her aunt.

"It's been great!" she grinned. "You know, all the animals liked me. I've made ever such a lot of friends."

"I know," said her aunt grimly. "They've all followed you home! Look behind you!"

Rhiannon thought it was funny at first, but when her aunt made her give *all* the animals their tea and take them all back to their homes before she had anything to eat herself, she promised should would never, ever leave a gate open again. And she never has.

Leave Those Leaves!

The twins were helping Mamma in the garden. It was a beautiful day, with brown and orange leaves swirling from the trees. Mamma was sweeping leaves off the paths. She had made a big pile beside the shed. It was a terrible temptation to the twins.

"Alfie, don't you dare!" called Mamma, as she spotted her son about to jump into the pile in his red boots.

"No, Mamma," called Alfie.

A moment later, Mamma spotted a little figure in a pink coat shuffling towards the pile. "Angie, I would be very cross!" she cried.

"Yes, Mamma," said Angie.

Faintly, through the window, they all heard the telephone ring in the house.

"I'll only be a minute," said Mamma.

Mamma's minute seemed very long to the twins. They sat on the bench and swung their legs for a while. Angie's boots fell off, but she put them on again. Alfie's boots wouldn't accidentally fall off whatever he tried.

At last, they couldn't bear it any more. "Shall we?" said Alfie.

"Ready, steady, go!" yelled Angie.

Holding hands, they ran towards the pile and jumped right into the middle. Then they tumbled and tossed until they were tired and lay down for a rest.

"Ouch, something's sticking into me," said Angie. She rummaged about. It was Mamma's ring! It must have fallen off as she worked.

The next moment, there was a thunderous rumble and a kind of snorting. "Are you cross, Mamma?" asked Alfie.

Mamma glared down at them. She was just about to give the two a piece of her mind when Angie handed her the ring.

A big struggle went on in Mamma's face. Then she smiled. "It would have been awful to lose this," she said. "Much more awful than clearing up leaves. Now, I must be very careful not to lose this ring again, so I'd better keep my hands in my pockets. Carry on, team!"

Index of Themes